Ed & Fred Flea

Pamela Duncan Edwards

Illustrated by Henry Cole

Hyperion Books for Children
NEW YORK

Printed in Mexico
This book is set in 18/30-point Giovanni Bold.
The artwork for each picture was prepared using watercolor and colored pencils.

First Edition
1 3 5 7 9 10 8 6 4 2

Library of Congress Cataloging-in-Publication Data
Edwards, Pamela Duncan.
Ed & Fred Flea/Pamela Duncan Edwards; illustrated by Henry Cole.
p. cm.
Summary: As his brother prepares to leave the dog they share, Fred the greedy flea pretends
to have the flu in order to stay behind and have the whole dog, unaware of the fate that awaits him.
ISBN O-7868-O468-8 (trade)—ISBN O-7868-2410-7 (lib. bdg.)
[1. Fleas—Fiction. 2. Greed—Fiction. 3. Dogs—Fiction. 4. Stories in rhyme.]
I. Cole, Henry, 1955- ill. II. Title. III. Title: Ed and Fred Flea.
PZ8.3.E283Ed 1999
[E]—DC21 98-42650

For Robert, remembering the gift of Angus! —P. D. E.

To Collie, Biscuit, White Kitty, Flounder, Miss Ann, Feather, Imp, Queenie, Longtail, Dirty Face, Peanut, Renoir, Trane, Collie Junior, Mullet, Seymour, Hobo, Nipper, Jake, Sam, Penny, Wing, Stinky, Mosby, Jack, Whitey, Moonshot, Bucky, Jet, Happy, Mosey, Keekee, Stuart, Caesar, Conrad, Spook, Irving, Tammy, Augie, Samantha, and Phoebe, with a lifetime of love. —H. N. C.

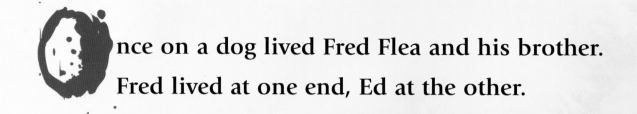
nce on a dog lived Fred Flea and his brother. Fred lived at one end, Ed at the other.

As small fleas they'd always found it a riddle:
If they each owned one end
then who owned . . .

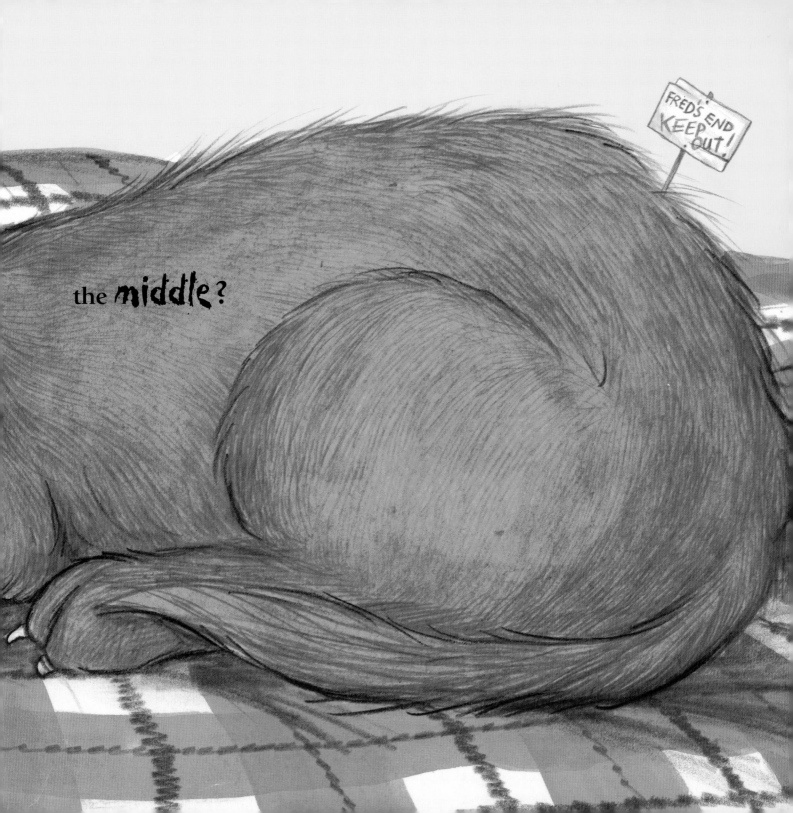

Ed was content with the bit that he had,

but Fred wanted it **all**, for he was selfish and bad.

Ed came one day with some terrible news.
"We'd better move on. I've been noticing clues!
The dog's **scratching** madly and I think it's a sign.
Something is up when he starts to whine."

Bad Fred saw his chance: "Stop that hullabaloo.
I really can't go, for I'm sick with the flu."

"But," replied Ed, "you're not coughing or shaking.
You don't have a fever. Are you sure you're not faking?"
"No, it's true!" Bad Fred lied. "And there never can be,
a pill to cure a poor flu-y flea.

"There are certainly mixtures for a camel with mumps,

that soon would get rid of his lumps and his bumps.

"There are certainly syrups to give to a snake when he's slithering around with a bad **stomachache**.

"There are plenty of medicines for families of weasels,
as **spot** by **spot** they come down with the measles.

"And we all know of tablets that come in a box,
that are swallowed by hens when they've got
chicken pox.

"But there's nothing, just nothing, you know it is true,
that can come to the aid of a flea with the flu!"

"You really must come," pleaded Ed. "You must try."

But Bad Fred, the phony, pretended to cry.

"Flee!" warned a fly.
"Fly!" begged Ed Flea.

"Go!" sobbed Bad Fred.

"Don't worry about me."

"Mayday! Mayday!" called a tick as it fled. **"Abandon dog! Danger ahead!"**

Then Ed Flea and the tick left the dog with a bound.

"Hurrah!" cried Bad Fred. "I've got all of the hound!

"And I don't have the flu. I'm not really sick.
They were all of them fools to believe in my trick.
I'm fit as a fiddle," he sang louder and louder. . . .

And that's when they dusted the dog with

Flea powder!

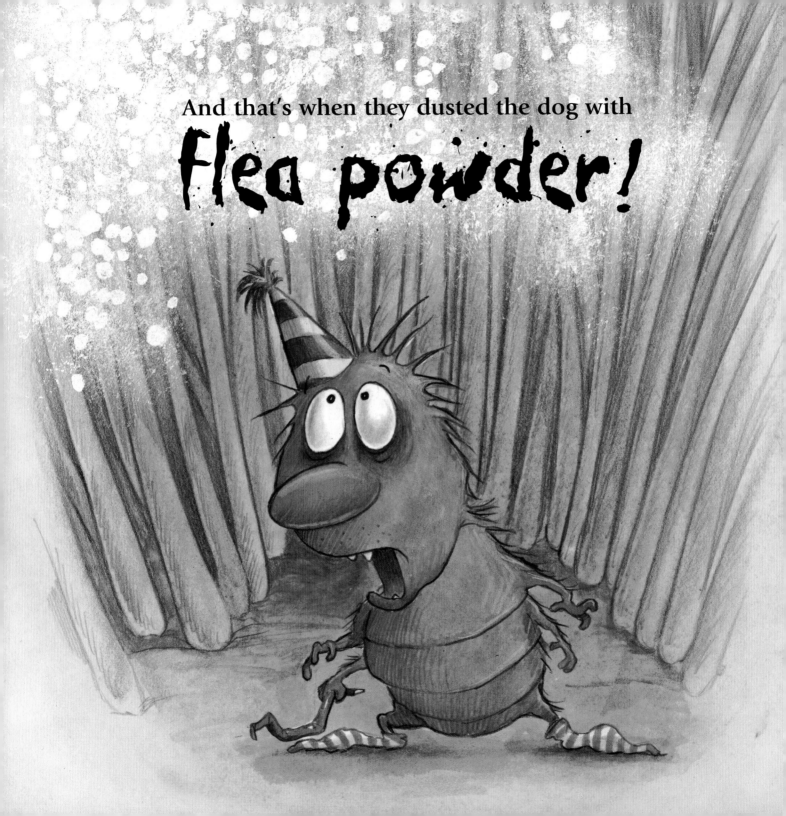

THE END